W9-CFB-801

It's Oregon or bust for the
Peanuts Pioneers!

Little Patriot Press® is a registered trademark of Salem Communications Holding Corporation

Cataloging-in-Publication data on file with the Library of Congress
ISBN 978-1-62157-344-9

Published in the United States by
Little Patriot Press
An imprint of Regnery Publishing
A Division of Salem Media Group
300 New Jersey Ave NW
Washington, DC 20001
www.RegneryKids.com
www.Peanuts.com

Manufactured in the United States of America
10 9 8 7 6 5 4 3 2 1

Books are available in quantity for promotional or premium use. For information on discounts and terms, please visit our website: www.Regnery.com.

Distributed to the trade by
Perseus Distribution
250 West 57th Street
New York, NY 10107

Westward Ho, Charlie Brown!

Peanuts created by **Charles M. Schulz**

Written by **Tracy Stratford** Illustrated by **Tom Brannon**

Little Patriot Press

"Hey, everyone! What do you want to play today?"
Charlie Brown asked his friends.

Who knew that one question could have so many answers? "Good grief!" he sighed.

"Look! Snoopy wants to play pioneers! Let's play that!"
Franklin cheered.

"Pioneers! Great idea!" said Peppermint Patty.
"Pioneers were adventurous people," Linus said.

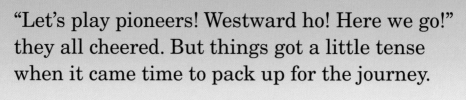

"Let's play pioneers! Westward ho! Here we go!" they all cheered. But things got a little tense when it came time to pack up for the journey.

Sally picked Linus to ride with her. "Come along, my sweet babboo," she cooed.

WHERE'S MY BLANKET?

Pigpen volunteered to be the wagon master. Who better to blaze the dusty trail?

"Giddyup, wagon train!" Pigpen shouted. The travelers took turns walking and riding in the wagons. "Westward ho! On we go!" Sally hollered.

OREGON OR BUST!

"Easy for you to say, Sally," Linus grumbled as he pulled Sally's wagon. "This isn't going to be all fun and games, you know."

He continued, "America's pioneers left their homes, friends, and families behind and headed west into the wild frontier. Did you hear me? Wild frontier!"

"This trip would be a lot quicker if we took the expressway!" Lucy said.

But Franklin explained, "There were no expressways back then! They traveled on rough dirt roads. Remember learning about those famous explorers Lewis and Clark and the fur traders who followed? They cleared the way for the Oregon Trail."

"I'm getting hungry," Charlie Brown said. "Does anyone see a drive-through?"

"Good luck with that, Chuck," Peppermint Patty said. "Everyone knows pioneers ate what they brought from home or what they caught along the way."

"Chow time!" Chef Marcie called out. "All the beans and bacon you can eat."

"No one said anything about walking so much," Lucy complained.

"Pioneers had to keep their wagons light so the oxen didn't wear out," Linus explained.

"Oxen? What about me?" Lucy whined. "My feet hurt so much it's making me crabby!"

The sun was setting when Pigpen announced, "Circle the wagons! It's time to make camp for the night."

"Sure hope they left the lights on for us," Franklin said.

But there were no lights, no cozy beds, no hot showers. There was a lot more work to do setting up tents, washing clothes, making campfires, and preparing meals.

After everyone finished dinner,
Schroeder started playing his piano.

Snoopy pulled out his fiddle and joined in.

There was a lot of foot-stomping, toe-tapping, and whirling and twirling going on around the campfire. Lucy even forgot about her sore feet!

"Great progress today, fellow pioneers," Linus said. "If we keep up this pace, we'll make it in a few months."

"You can't be serious!" Lucy said.

"What did you expect?" Franklin asked. "Covered wagons only traveled 20 miles on a good day. Remember, their destination was more than 2,000 miles away."

"This pillow feels like a rock!" Lucy whined.

"Quit kicking me!" Schroeder shouted.

"That wasn't me," Franklin said.

Suddenly, they heard howling in the hills.

Marcie asked, "What's that noise? Is it just me, or is it a little scary out here?"

"Where's our guard dog Snoopy?" Sally asked.

The howling was enough to send everybody running.

"I'm done playing pioneer!" Pigpen shouted, as he and the others raced home.

"Homeward bound!" yelled Charlie Brown.
"Those pioneers sure were brave."

Who Became a Pioneer?

There were many reasons why people became pioneers and headed west in the 19th century, especially after the Louisiana Purchase in 1803 and the Lewis and Clark expedition that mapped it. People who lived in the increasingly crowded East heard stories about opportunities to create a better life in the West. In 1848, gold was discovered in California, and in 1862, Congress passed the Homestead Act to encourage western settlement. This law allowed a person or family to earn complete ownership of a 160-acre parcel of land by building a home and growing crops or raising animals on the property. They paid a fee of $10 to record their claim.

Travel

Most pioneers made their way west in organized groups of "wagon trains." Wagon trains could have over 100 wagons traveling together. Pioneers liked small wagons called "prairie schooners." Many pioneers started out in Missouri, which became known as the "Gateway to the West." Pioneers traveled on such famous roads as the Santa Fe Trail, the Smoky Hill Trail, and the Oregon Trail, which was more than 2,000 miles long. Though wagon trains often formed in a line, when they came to wide-open spaces the wagons would often fan out and travel side by side to minimize kicking up dust. Depending on weather, river and mountain crossings, and other challenges, a wagon train usually traveled 10 to 20 miles a day. Most journeys took several months.

A typical day started with a wake-up call at 4 a.m. Everyone needed time to prepare for the day's travel, which usually started at 7 a.m. and ended around 4 p.m. When they stopped to set up camp, the drivers would form a circle with their wagons to keep their animals safe inside. The families cooked and tended to chores while the animals grazed. Sometimes the pioneers sang or played music and danced before turning in for the night.

Life Out West

If a pioneer survived the trip out west, finding land was easy. But building a home and farming the land were hard! On the plains, there were few trees or hills for protection, especially from the bright summer sun and the cold winter wind and snow. Without trees, there was no wood to build houses. Some pioneers built houses partly underground in the dirt or "sod," cutting out blocks of hard earth from the grassy prairie to make these sod houses. Dark, dirty, and cold, sod houses became muddy when it rained. There was little fuel for cooking and heating. Whatever the pioneers could find to burn, they used: dried grass, small plants, even cow and buffalo dung. Lack of water was also a problem. Many months could pass without rain, and families could lose all their crops. When the railroads came west, they brought wood, coal, and other important materials to the settlers.

The world's first transcontinental railroad was built between 1863 and 1869 to join the eastern and western halves of the United States. It linked the railway network of the East Coast with the rapidly growing western region of the country. The transcontinental railroad is considered to be one of the greatest technological feats of the 19th century. When it was completed, it was called the Pacific Railroad. It served as a vital link for travel, trade, and commerce and opened up vast new territory for settlement.